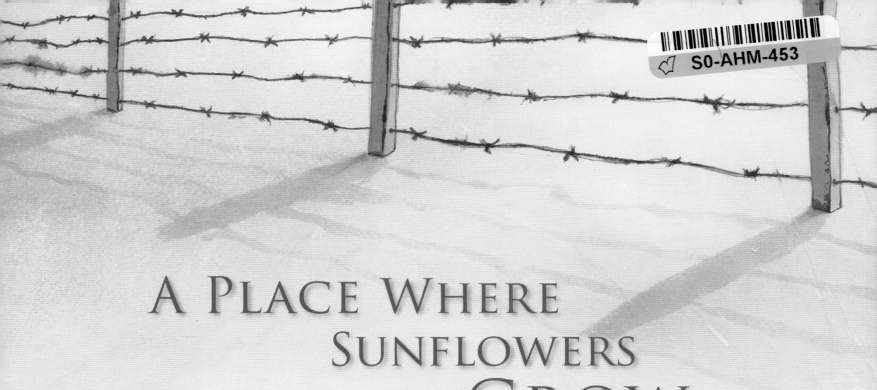

A Place Where Sunflowers Grow

砂漠に咲いたひまわり

Story / 作家:

Amy Lee-Tai

Illustrations / 挿絵:

Felicia Hoshino

Children's Book Press
AN IMPRINT OF Lee & Low Books Inc.
New York

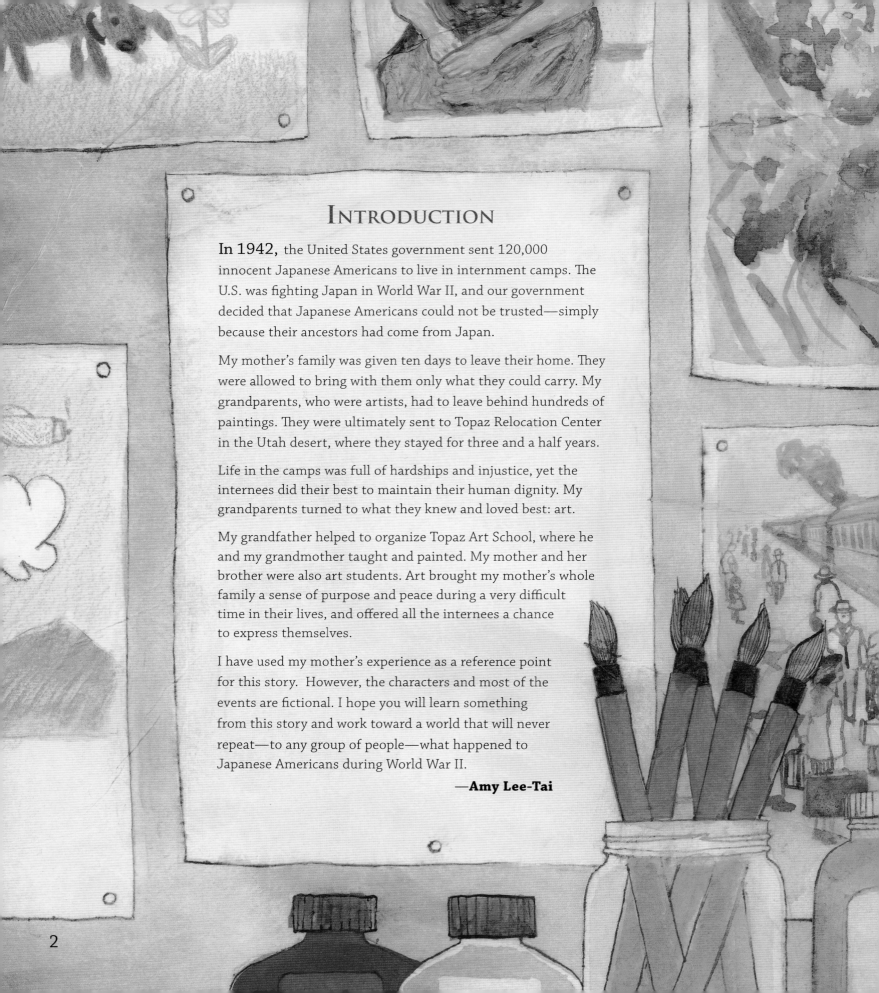

INTRODUCTION

In 1942, the United States government sent 120,000 innocent Japanese Americans to live in internment camps. The U.S. was fighting Japan in World War II, and our government decided that Japanese Americans could not be trusted—simply because their ancestors had come from Japan.

My mother's family was given ten days to leave their home. They were allowed to bring with them only what they could carry. My grandparents, who were artists, had to leave behind hundreds of paintings. They were ultimately sent to Topaz Relocation Center in the Utah desert, where they stayed for three and a half years.

Life in the camps was full of hardships and injustice, yet the internees did their best to maintain their human dignity. My grandparents turned to what they knew and loved best: art.

My grandfather helped to organize Topaz Art School, where he and my grandmother taught and painted. My mother and her brother were also art students. Art brought my mother's whole family a sense of purpose and peace during a very difficult time in their lives, and offered all the internees a chance to express themselves.

I have used my mother's experience as a reference point for this story. However, the characters and most of the events are fictional. I hope you will learn something from this story and work toward a world that will never repeat—to any group of people—what happened to Japanese Americans during World War II.

—Amy Lee-Tai

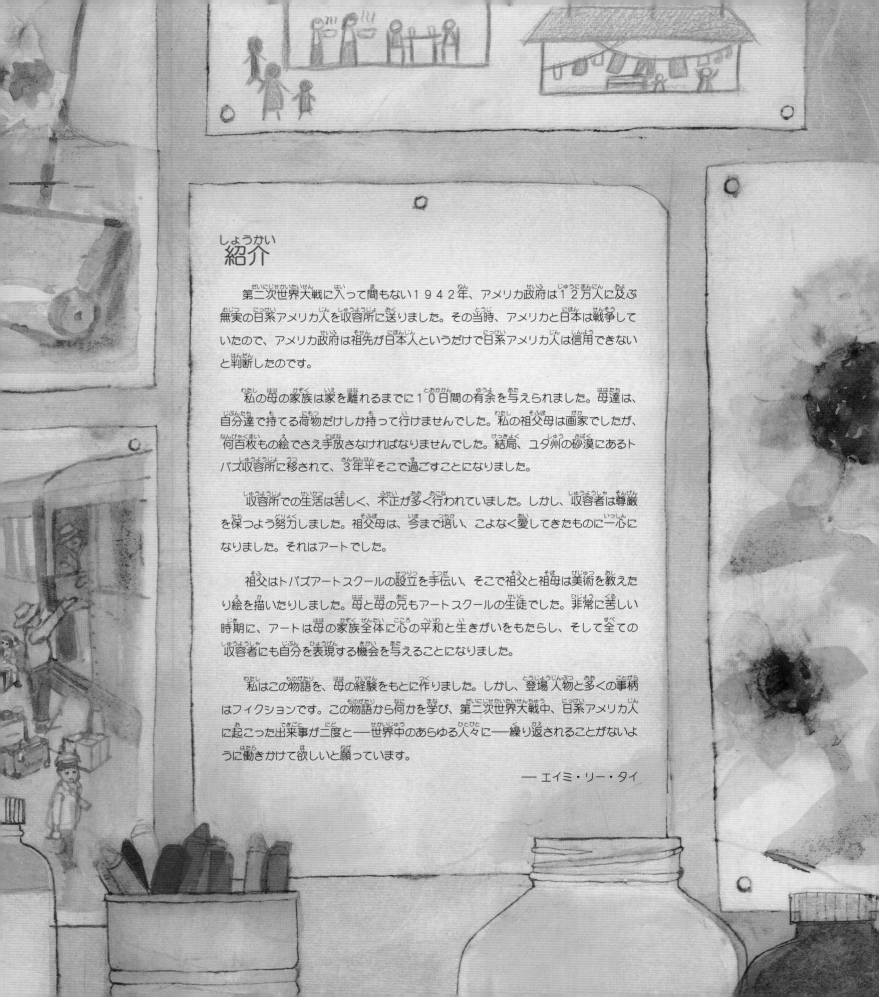

紹介

　第二次世界大戦に入って間もない１９４２年、アメリカ政府は１２万人に及ぶ無実の日系アメリカ人を収容所に送りました。その当時、アメリカと日本は戦争していたので、アメリカ政府は祖先が日本人というだけで日系アメリカ人は信用できないと判断したのです。

　私の母の家族は家を離れるまでに１０日間の有余を与えられました。母達は、自分達で持てる荷物だけしか持って行けませんでした。私の祖父母は画家でしたが、何百枚もの絵でさえ手放さなければなりませんでした。結局、ユタ州の砂漠にあるトパズ収容所に移されて、３年半そこで過ごすことになりました。

　収容所での生活は苦しく、不正が多く行われていました。しかし、収容者は尊厳を保つよう努力しました。祖父母は、今まで培い、こよなく愛してきたものに一心になりました。それはアートでした。

　祖父はトパズアートスクールの設立を手伝い、そこで祖父と祖母は美術を教えたり絵を描いたりしました。母と母の兄もアートスクールの生徒でした。非常に苦しい時期に、アートは母の家族全体に心の平和と生きがいをもたらし、そして全ての収容者にも自分を表現する機会を与えることになりました。

　私はこの物語を、母の経験をもとに作りました。しかし、登場人物と多くの事柄はフィクションです。この物語から何かを学び、第二次世界大戦中、日系アメリカ人に起こった出来事が二度と——世界中のあらゆる人々に——繰り返されることがないように働きかけて欲しいと願っています。

　　　　　　　　　　　　　　　　　　　　　　— エイミ・リー・タイ

Mari stared at the ground. It had only been a week since she and her mother had planted a handful of sunflower seeds outside their new home. Mari asked Mama, "Will these flowers grow as tall and strong and beautiful as the ones in our old backyard?"

"It will take time, patience, and care," Mama replied gently. *"Sabaku ni hana wa sodachinikui no yo."*

"Flowers don't grow easily in the desert," Mari repeated in English. She glared at the sand like the hot May sun, as if that might make the seeds spring to life. But all she saw were dry grains of sand.

マリは足下の土をじっと見つめました。マリがお母さんと一緒に、新しい家の前に一握りのひまわりの種を時いてから、まだ1週間しか経っていません。「この花は、昔の家の裏庭の花と同じように高く伸びて、力強く、美しくなるの？」

マリはママに尋ねました。「時間をかけて、辛抱強く、世話をすることが必要よ。砂漠に花は育ちにくいのよ。」ママは優しい声で答えました。「Flowers don't grow easily in the desert.」マリは英語で言いました。

まるで種に生命を吹き込むかのように、マリは5月の太陽のような熱いまなざしで土を見つめました。しかし、そこにはただざらざらとした乾いた砂があるだけでした。

As she watered the seeds, Mari thought about her family's little house in California. Her parents, who were artists, would paint while Mari and her older brother Kenji played alongside them in their flower-filled backyard.

Had it only been thirteen months since they were forced to leave? First they had to live in a horse stall that smelled of manure in Tanforan, California. Now they were living in a tarpaper barrack in Topaz, Utah. Everything but her family had been taken from Mari—and she hadn't done anything wrong!

"Mari-chan, it's three o'clock, time for art school." Papa's tender voice pulled Mari back to reality. "Let's not be late. *Ikoo, ne!*"

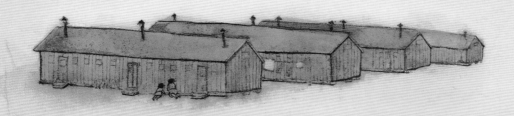

種に水をやりながら、マリはカリフォルニア州での小さな家をなつかしく思い出しました。マリとケンジお兄さんが花の溢れた裏庭で遊んでいるかたわらで、画家の両親は絵を描いていました。

家を離れてから１３カ月しか経っていないなんて――。最初は、カリフォルニア州タンフランで肥料臭い馬屋に住まなければなりませんでした。今は、ユタ州トパズでタール紙でできた兵舎に住んでいます。マリは家族以外の全てを失いました。悪いことを何もしていないのに！

「マリちゃん、３時になったよ。アートスクールが始まるよ！遅刻しないように行こう、ね！」パパの優しい声はマリを現実に引き戻しました。

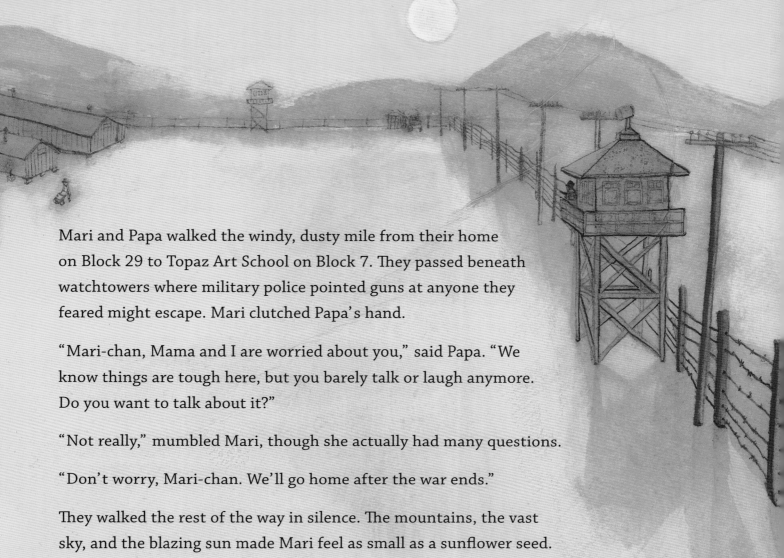

Mari and Papa walked the windy, dusty mile from their home on Block 29 to Topaz Art School on Block 7. They passed beneath watchtowers where military police pointed guns at anyone they feared might escape. Mari clutched Papa's hand.

"Mari-chan, Mama and I are worried about you," said Papa. "We know things are tough here, but you barely talk or laugh anymore. Do you want to talk about it?"

"Not really," mumbled Mari, though she actually had many questions.

"Don't worry, Mari-chan. We'll go home after the war ends."

They walked the rest of the way in silence. The mountains, the vast sky, and the blazing sun made Mari feel as small as a sunflower seed.

マリとパパは、２９ブロックにある家から７ブロックのトパズアートスクールまで強風とほこりの中１マイルを歩いて行きました。２人は兵隊が立っている監視塔の下を通りました。兵隊は逃げるおそれのある収容者にライフルを向けるのです。マリはパパの手を強く握りました。

「マリちゃん、パパとママはあなたのことを心配しているんだよ。ここでの生活が大変だということは分かるけど、最近マリちゃんはあまり喋ったり笑ったりしない。何か話したいことがあるんじゃないの？」パパは言いました。「ううん・・・。」

マリはもじもじ答えました。でも、本当は聞きたいことがたくさんありました。

「心配しないで、マリちゃん。戦争が終わったらカリフォルニアへ帰るからね。」

２人はアートスクールまで静かに歩いて行きました。遠い山、広大な空、照りつける太陽は、マリ自身をひまわりの種ほど小さく感じさせました。

At Topaz Art School, Papa brought Mari to her classroom, then went next door to teach the adult sketching class. Mari had hoped to see some friends in class, but didn't recognize anyone.

Mrs. Hanamoto passed out paper and crayons. She said, "For our first class, have fun and draw whatever you want." Mari listened to the tapping and swishing of crayons at the other desks. She thought long and hard, but her paper was still blank as class ended.

A few students shared their drawings with the class. Janie drew the pet dog she had left behind. Eddie drew his three cousins who had been sent to a camp in Idaho. Aiko drew different places in Topaz: the mess hall, the latrine, the laundry room.

Mari enjoyed the other drawings, but wished she had one of her own to share.

トパズアートスクールで、パパはマリを子供向けの教室に連れて行って、それから隣の大人のためのスケッチ教室へ教えに行きました。マリは教室で友達に会えたらいいなぁと思っていたけれども、知っている子は1人も見当たりませんでした。

ハナモト先生は紙とクレヨンを渡しました。「最初のクラスでは、楽しく好きなものを描きましょう。」マリの周りの机から、クレヨンをすらすらと走らせる軽快な音が聞こえてきました。マリは一生懸命 考えましたが、クラスが終わった時、紙はまだ真っ白でした。

何人かの子供は自分の絵をみんなに見せました。ジェイニーは、家においてきたペットの犬を描きました。エディは、アイダホ州に送られた3人の従兄を描きました。アイコは、トパズでの3つの場所——食堂とお手洗いと洗濯室——を描きました。

他の生徒の絵は面白かったけれども、マリも自分の絵を描いて見てもらいたいなぁと思いました。

11

Since Papa had another class to teach, Mari walked by herself to the mess hall. Mama and Kenji met her outside.

Passing through the mess hall doorway was like turning up the volume on a radio. Utensils clanged, people talked, babies cried. Mari cringed at the noise. The family took their place in the long dinner line, and Papa joined them just before they received their portion of food.

As they sat down, Papa asked, "Mari-chan, how was your first class?"

"I couldn't think of anything to draw," said Mari.

"That happens to me sometimes, too," Papa replied.

"Really?" asked Mari. "Even though you're an artist?"

"Yes," Papa smiled, "but I don't give up."

パパはもう1つのクラスがあったので、マリは食堂まで1人で歩いて行きました。外でママとケンジと待ち合わせました。

食堂に入ると、中はまるでラジオの音を大きくしたような騒騒しさでした。フォークとナイフがカンカンと鳴ったり、人々が話し合ったり、赤ちゃんが泣いていたりしていました。マリは雑音で怖気づきました。3人は夕食をもらうための長い列に並びました。食事を受け取る直前にパパがやってきました。

テーブルにすわりながら、パパはマリに聞きました。

「マリちゃん、最初のクラスはどうだった？」

「描くものが思いつかなかったわ。」マリは言いました。

「パパも時々そうだよ。」　「本当？パパは画家なのに？」マリは聞きました。

「そうだよ。でもね、思いつくまであきらめないよ。」パパはほほ笑みました。

13

The morning of the next art class, Mari and Mama waited in the long line at the latrine. The toilet and shower stalls had no doors. Mari and Mama tried to avoid looking at the other women and girls.

Mama asked, "Mari-chan, are you worried about today's class?"

Mari nodded. She had been wondering what Mrs. Hanamoto would ask her to draw.

"Remember Papa's advice. You will be able to draw, just like your sunflowers will be able to grow."

次の絵のクラスの日の朝、ママとマリはお手洗いの行列で待っていました。お手洗いとシャワーの個室にはドアがなかったので、マリとママは他の女の人達を見ないようにしました。

「マリちゃん、今日の絵のクラスを心配しているの？」 ママは聞きました。

マリはうなずきました。ハナモト先生は何を描かせるかなとマリは考えていました。

「パパの言ったことを思い出してね。マリちゃんは必ず描ける。マリちゃんのひまわりが咲くのと同じよ。」

That afternoon, Mrs. Hanamoto told the class, "Draw something that makes you happy at Topaz." Again, Mari struggled for an idea. Then Mrs. Hanamoto appeared at her desk.

"Mari-chan, I noticed that you didn't draw anything in our last class. Some other students also had a hard time."

"I wasn't the only one?" Mari answered hopefully.

"No, it happens quite often. You just have to keep trying. Now, what are you going to draw?"

"I can't think of anything that makes me happy at Topaz."

"Then draw something that made you happy *before* you came here," suggested Mrs. Hanamoto.

その日の午後、ハナモト先生はみんなに言いました。

「トパズでの楽しいことを描きましょう。」

この日もまた、マリはいい考えがなかなか思いつきませんでした。ハナモト先生はマリの机に来ました。「マリちゃん、この前のクラスで何も描かなかったわね。他にもマリちゃんのように描けなかった生徒もいたのよ。」

「私だけではなかったの？」マリはうれしく応えました。

「そうよ。よくあることよ。あきらめないことが必要。さあ、何を描く？」

「トパズで楽しいことは思いつかないの。」

「じゃあ、トパズに来る前の楽しいことを描いたら？」

ハナモト先生はそうすすめました。

今度はマリはすぐに思いつきました。カリフォルニアの家の裏庭です！マリは絵を
描き始めました。パパが作ってくれたブランコ、ママが植えた桜の木、色とりどり
の庭。ハナモト先生が授業がそろそろ終わると告げにやってきた時も、マリはまだ
夢中で描いていました。

マリは隣に座っているアイコが自分の絵を見ていることに気付きました。アイコは
ささやきました。「マリちゃんの裏庭ってとても楽しそうね。」

マリは小さな声で答えました。「カリフォルニアの家に帰れたら、遊びに来てね。」

This time, Mari knew right away—her backyard in California!

She drew the swing that Papa had built, the *sakura* tree that Mama had planted, and the garden with its rainbow of colors. She was still busy drawing when Mrs. Hanamoto announced that class was almost over.

Mari noticed that Aiko, who sat next to her, was looking at her picture. Aiko whispered, "Your backyard looks like a lot of fun."

Mari whispered back, "Maybe you can visit when we all go home."

Mari walked home as quickly as she could. She burst into her family's barrack.

"How was art class, Mari-chan?" asked Mama, expecting only a quiet reply.

But Mari answered quickly, "Mrs. Hanamoto is nice and I got to use crayons and I drew this picture!"

"It's our old backyard!" exclaimed Kenji.

Mama smiled. "It's lovely. Why don't we hang it up?"

Sunlight streamed through the open barrack door. Mari hung her drawing on the bare wall above her bed. It added a little cheer to their dark, one-room home, even when it was time to close the door.

マリはできるだけ速く歩いて帰りました。そして家族のいる兵舎に駆け込みました。

「マリちゃん、絵のクラスはどうだった？」ママは元気のない返事しか返ってこないだろうと思いながら尋ねました。

しかし、マリはすぐ答えました。「ハナモト先生は優しかったよ。クレヨンを使ったの。それでこの絵を描いたのよ！」

「僕達の裏庭だ！」ケンジは大きな声を出しました。ママはにこにこしました。「素敵な絵。壁にかけましょう！」兵舎の開けっ放しの玄関から太陽の光が入ってきました。マリはベッドのわきの何もない壁に絵をかけました。ドアが閉まっていても、その絵は部屋が１つしかない家を少しだけ明るくしました。

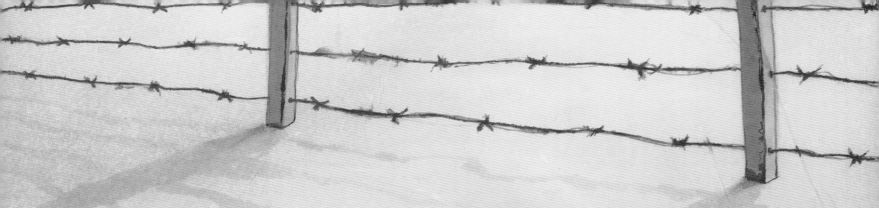

Every Wednesday and Sunday, Mari and Papa walked together to art school. Hand in hand, they shared peaceful, silent moments.

Mari began to ask Papa questions: "Why are we in camp? Why is almost everyone here Japanese American? Will I ever see my old friends again?"

He and Mama had resigned themselves to the internment, but Papa tried his best to answer. He turned to Japanese philosophy, noting the cycle of life: "Spring comes after winter, and flowers bloom again. Peace comes after war. Try not to worry, Mari-chan."

It was as if, with every drawing she created, Mari found another question to ask and the courage to ask it.

毎週 水曜日と日曜日、マリとパパはアートスクールに歩いて行きました。手を繋いで、2人は穏やかで静かなひと時を過ごしました。

ある日、マリはパパに尋ねました。「どうして私達は収容所にいるの？どうしてほとんどみんなは日系アメリカ人なの？昔の友達とはまた会えるの？」

パパとママは収容所に入ることを余儀なくされました。でもパパはできる限りの質問に答えました。パパは日本の哲学にある物の移り変わりを取り上げて、マリに話しました。

「冬の後には、春が来て、花がまた咲く。戦争の後には、平和が来る。マリちゃん、心配しないで。」

マリは新しい絵を描くたびに、次から次へと聞きたいことがわいてきて、それと共にそれを聞く勇気も出てくるかのようでした。

One day after class, Aiko asked Mari, "Do you want to walk home together? My family lives on Block 40."

"Sure, that sounds like fun," replied Mari. "Besides, those guardsmen scare me."

"Me, too," agreed Aiko. "Do they have to carry guns?"

As they walked and talked, Mari and Aiko didn't notice the sky begin to darken and the wind begin to blow. Suddenly, a wall of dirt, twigs, and sagebrush roots rushed toward them, stinging their skin.

"Dust storm!" shouted Aiko, grabbing Mari's hand. They tried to run, but it was difficult to move or see anything in the heavy, dirty wind.

ある日、クラスが終わった後、アイコはマリに聞きました。

「一緒に歩いて帰らない？私達家族は４０ブロックに住んでいるのよ。」

「いいよ。面白そうね。」　マリは答えました。　　「あの兵隊達も恐いし…。」

「私も。」　　「あの人達は銃を持たないといけないのかな？」

マリとアイコは歩きながら話している間に、空が暗くなって、風が吹き出したこと
に気付きませんでした。突然、砂と小枝とヨモギの根っ子が混じった風が彼女達
に向かって、肌を突き刺すように吹きつけました。

「砂嵐だ！」　　アイコは叫んで、マリの手をつかみました。走ろうとしたけれど、
強い砂嵐の中で、何も見えず、身動きもできませんでした。

Together, they managed—very slowly—to make their way to Mari's barrack. They slammed the door and collapsed on the floor, coughing and gasping for air.

Mama rushed toward them. "Mari-chan! Aiko-chan! Are you all right?"

"We're fine, Mama," said Mari, covered in dirt from head to toe. She and Aiko burst out laughing, relieved to be safe and happy to be friends. From then on, they walked home together after every art class.

とてもゆっくりだったけれど、2人はなんとかマリの兵舎までたどり着きました。ドアをパタンと閉めて、2人は床に崩れて、咳をし、あえぎました。

ママが走って来ました。「マリちゃん、アイコちゃん、大丈夫？」

「私達は大丈夫よ、ママ。」頭からつま先までほこりだらけのマリは言いました。

マリとアイコは突然笑い転げました。無事に帰れたことにほっとしたし、また、友達同士であることがうれしかったからです。その日から、2人は絵のクラスが終わった後、一緒に帰るようになりました。

In August, during the last week of class, Mrs. Hanamoto said, "Today, create a drawing using different shapes."

Mari drew her family's barrack using rectangles, squares, and a triangle. Then she added circles, lines, and teardrop shapes. Her sunflowers!

She included Aiko and herself. The sunflowers towered above their heads so high they couldn't even reach them on their tiptoes!

For the first time, Mari volunteered to share her drawing with the class. As she spoke, she noticed Mrs. Hanamoto's and Aiko's smiling faces, as cheerful as the sunflowers in her drawing.

8月の下旬、クラスの最後の週に、ハナモト先生は言いました。

「今日は、いろんな形を使って絵を描きましょう。」

マリは、長方形と四角と三角で家族の兵舎を描きました。それから、円と線と涙の粒のような形を加えました。マリのひまわりでした！

自分とアイコも描きました。背伸びしても手が届かないほど、ひまわりは2人の背よりずっと高く伸びていました。

マリは初めて自分の絵をみんなに紹介しました。話しているうちに、ハナモト先生とアイコの笑顔が、マリが描いたひまわりのようににこやかなのに気付きました。

After class, Mari and Aiko walked home together. Mari looked at her new drawing and said, "I've watered my sunflower seeds every day for three months now. I wonder if my sunflowers are ever going to grow here."

Suddenly Aiko stopped and pointed and said, "You can stop wondering!"

Mari followed Aiko's finger to the side of Mari's barrack, where nine tiny green stems peeked through the ground.

"Mama! Kenji! Come see!" exclaimed Mari. She couldn't wait to show Papa when he got home.

To Mari, seeing the little seedlings was like seeing old friends again. In that moment, her old life, and whatever her new life would be like after the war, didn't feel so far away.

クラスの後、マリとアイコは歩いて帰りました。マリは、今日描いた絵を見て言いました。「３ヵ月間、私は毎日ひまわりの種に水をやってきたの。ここでは、私のひまわりはいつか咲くかな。」突然、アイコは立ち止まって指を差しました。「心配しなくていいよ！」

マリはアイコが指差す先に目をやりました。マリの兵舎のわきに９つの緑の芽が土からそっと出ていました。

「ママ、ケンジ、見に来て！」マリは大きな声で叫びました。

マリはパパの帰りを待ち切れませんでした。

マリにとって、芽を見ることは、幼なじみに再会することと同じでした。その瞬間、マリは以前の生活からこれからの戦後の生活がどのように変わっても、明るく元気に生きていけると感じたのでした。

At Topaz, my grandmother Hisako Hibi and my mother Ibuki Hibi Lee really did plant sunflower seeds, and my mother tended to them faithfully. During the summer of 1943, the sunflowers grew about eight feet high, to the top of the barrack wall. Other internees would often stop and admire how they brightened the barren landscape. The flowers were also used by art students as models and by floral arrangement students in their displays.

The war—and the internment—ended in 1945. In 1988, the U.S. Government finally apologized to the surviving internees from the camps. It admitted that the internment was due to racial prejudice, war-time paranoia, and poor leadership. The government also acknowledged that no Japanese American was ever found guilty of endangering the U.S. during World War II.

—Amy Lee-Tai

Photo by Peter S. Lee

Amy Lee-Tai, who is of Japanese and Chinese ancestry, was born in Queens, New York. She first learned about the Japanese American internment from her mother and through her grandmother's paintings. After earning her Master's in Education from Harvard, she worked in schools as a Reading Specialist for eight years. She lives in Virginia with her husband and two daughters. This is her first book.

To all Japanese Americans who were interned during World War II, for your courage and grace. —ALT

Photo by Yoshi Hoshino

Felicia Hoshino was born in San Francisco, California. A graduate of the California College of the Arts, she is a prize-winning, full-time artist and illustrator. In addition to creating mixed-media images for children's books and magazines such as *Cicada*, Felicia also studies and performs Japanese classical dance. She and her husband and son live in San Francisco, California.

In dedication to my grandparents: Minoru and Chizuko Arikawa (Poston, AZ) and Tervo and Dorothy Umino (Minidoka, ID); and to our newest love, Sora. —FH

A note about the artwork: The illustrations for this book were created with watercolor, ink, tissue paper, and acrylic paint. Felicia based some of her compositions on artwork by Hisako Hibi, grandmother of the author and a prominent Japanese American painter. Children's Book Press is deeply grateful to Ibuki Hibi Lee for offering generous access to Hisako Hibi's sketches and artifacts during the making of this book. You can find more information on Hisako Hibi in her memoir, *Peaceful Painter*, published by Heydey Books.

Special thanks to Miho Ishida for her indispensable help with the Japanese translation, and to Etsuko Nogami, Keigo Morita, and Akiko Kitamura; Ina Cumpiano; Rosalyn Sheff; and the National Japanese American Historical Society.

Children's Book Press, an imprint of LEE & LOW BOOKS INC., 95 Madison Avenue, New York, NY 10016, leeandlow.com

Japanese translation by Marc Akio Lee
Japanese typesetting by Luna Concepts
Book design by Lorena Piñon, Pinwheel Design
Book production by The Kids at Our House

Library of Congress Cataloging-in-Publication Data
Lee-Tai, Amy, 1967-
A place where sunflowers grow = Sabaku ni saita himawari / story by Amy Lee-Tai; illustrations by Felicia Hoshino; [Japanese translation, Marc Akio Lee].
p.cm.
Summary: While she and her family are interned at Topaz Relocation Center during World War II, Mari gradually adjusts as she enrolls in an art class, makes a friend, plants sunflowers, and waits for them to grow.
ISBN 978-0-89239-215-5 (hc)　　ISBN 978-0-89239-274-2 (pb)
1. Japanese Americans—Evacuation and relocation, 1942-1945—Juvenile fiction. [1. Japanese Americans—Evacuation and relocation, 1942-1945—Fiction. 2. Japanese language materials—Bilingual.] I. Hoshino, Felicia, ill. II. Lee, Marc Akio. III. Title. IV. Title: Sabaku ni saita himawari.
PZ49.31.L44 2006 2014
[E]—dc22　　　　　　　　　　　　2005032957

Manufactured in China by Jade Productions, March 2014
HC 10　9　8　7　6　5
PB 10　9　8　7　6　5　4　3　2
First Edition